BEN

Cleans Up

written and illustrated by

Keren Ludlow and Willy Smax

Dolphin

IN THE SAME SERIES:

Benny and the Brass Band
Benny Goes to the Seaside
Benny and the Burst Pipe
Benny and the Bubble Car
Benny and the Big Fire
Benny and the Pony
Benny's Big Cousin

First published in Great Britain in 2000
as a Dolphin Paperback
by Orion Children's Books
a division of the Orion Publishing Group Ltd
Orion House, 5 Upper St Martin's Lane, London WC2H 9EA

A catalogue record for this book is available from the British Library
Printed in Italy
ISBN 1 85881 870 2

Mike McCannick was worried.

The Mayor was going to give a prize
for the cleanest building in Brummingham.

"There's lots of work to be done if we're going to win that prize," said Benny the Breakdown Truck as he washed the windows.

Mike swept up all the rubbish. But as soon as he had finished the wind came and blew it all away. Now everything was untidy again.

"This is hopeless," said Mike.

"We'll never win."

"Look," said Benny.

"Here comes Mr Duster-Buster, the street cleaner.
Perhaps he can help."

"Of course I'll help," said Mr Duster-Buster.

"Where would you like me to start?"

Just then, Morton the motorbike
came whizzing round the corner.
"Beep! Beep!" he hooted.

"**Aaah!**" shrieked Mr Duster-Buster.
He was so surprised that he shot out
a big cloud of dust all over Mike.

"Oh no!" said Mike.

"Hee hee!" went Morton, and he whizzed off again.

"Sorry about that," said
Mr Duster-Buster.
"Let me clean you up."
He sprayed Mike with warm water,
washed his face,
and brushed his shoes until they shone.
Then he started on the garage.

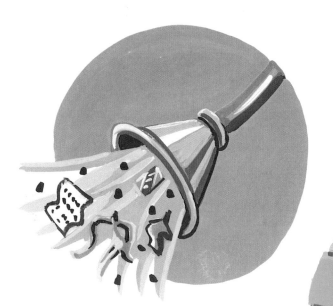

In no time at all ...

the rubbish
had disappeared,

and the windows
and petrol pumps
gleamed.

They all stood back to admire Smallbills Garage.

"It looks great," said Mike.

"We're bound to win the prize!" said Benny.

Just then Morton came roaring back
and beeped his horn. **"BEEP!"**

"Aaah!" shrieked Mr Duster-Buster.
"Oh no, not again!" said Benny.

The naughty blue motorbike
laughed so much that he burst an oil seal.
Mike was very cross with him.

"Don't worry," said Mr Duster-Buster.
And he quickly sucked up the oil
and polished Benny all over.

Mr Duster-Buster had just finished cleaning Benny when the Mayor's car pulled up.

"Welcome to Smallbills Garage," said Mike.

The Mayor and judges
checked the garage . . .

inside and out.

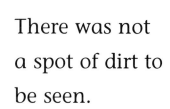

There was not
a spot of dirt to
be seen.

"Well done," said the Mayor.
"Smallbills Garage wins the prize for
Brummingham's cleanest building.
And Benny the Breakdown Truck wins the prize
for Brummingham's cleanest vehicle!"

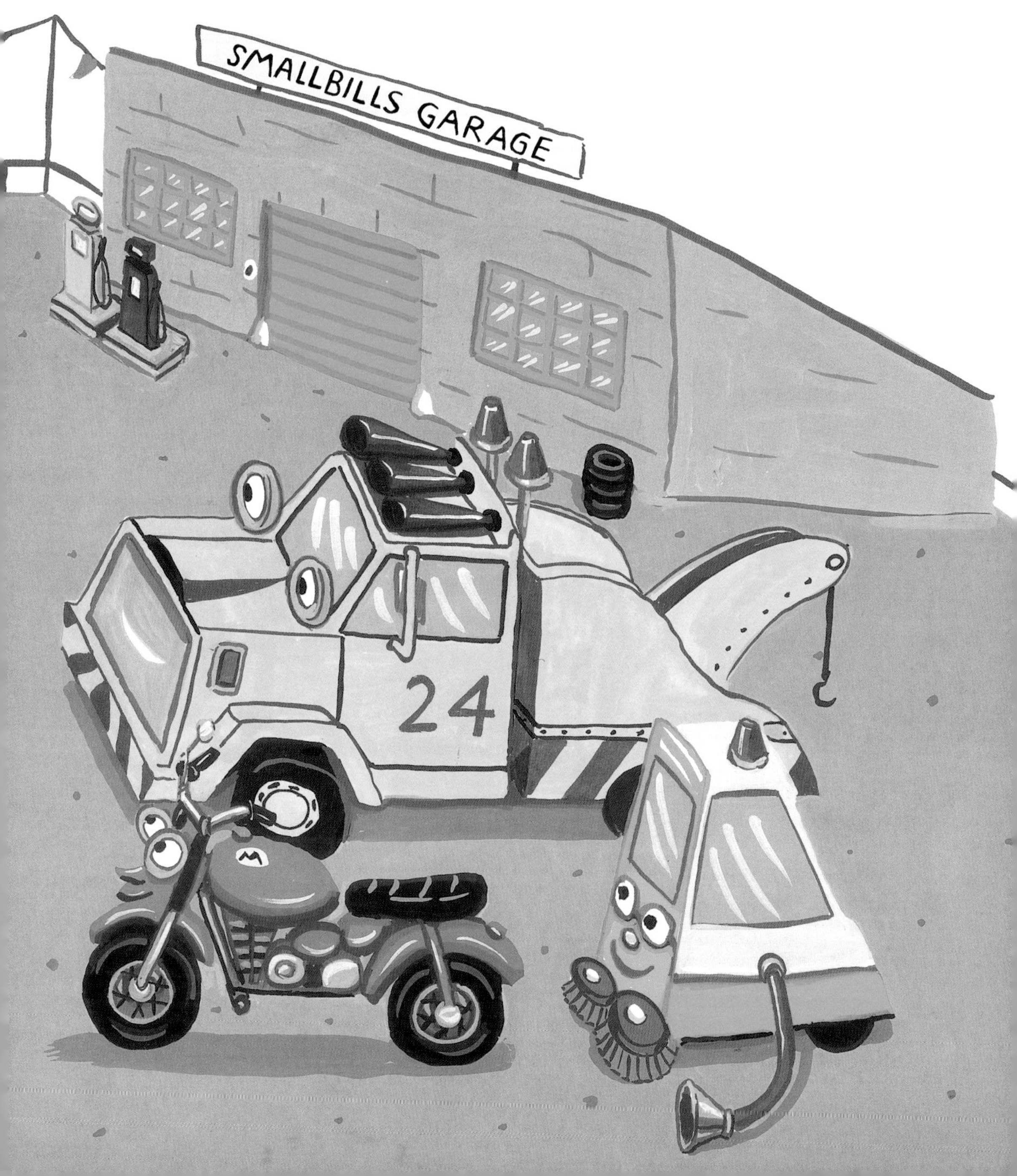
SMALLBILLS GARAGE
24

Benny was so pleased he sounded his horns
as loud as he could, "**B E E E E E P!**"

"**Aaah!**" shrieked Mr Duster-Buster.
And he covered Morton
in a big black cloud of oil.

"Oh dear," said the Mayor.
"I think I'd better give a prize to Morton, for being the dirtiest motorbike in Brummingham!"